Tug! Tug!

and

Lots of Spots

'Tug! Tug!' and 'Lots of Spots'
An original concept by Jenny Jinks
© Jenny Jinks

Illustrated by Daniela Dogliani

Published by MAVERICK ARTS PUBLISHING LTD

Studio 3A, City Business Centre, 6 Brighton Road,

Horsham, West Sussex, RH13 5BB

© Maverick Arts Publishing Limited May 2018

+44 (0)1403 256941

A CIP catalogue record for this book is available at the British Library.

ISBN 978-1-84886-344-6

www.maverickbooks.co.uk

Pink

This book is rated as: Pink Band (Guided Reading)
This story is decodable at Letters and Sounds Phase 2.

Tug! Tug!

and

Lots of Spots

By
Jenny Jinks

Illustrated by
Daniela Dogliani

The Letter Y

Trace the lower and upper case letter with a finger. Sound out the letter.

*Down,
around,
up,
down,
around*

*Down,
lift,
down,
down*

Some words to familiarise:

carrot   tug   Flop

High-frequency words:

has   a   the   it   and

Tips for Reading 'Tug! Tug!'

- Practise the words listed above before reading the story.

- If the reader struggles with any of the other words, ask them to look for sounds they know in the word. Encourage them to sound out the words and help them read the words if necessary.

- After reading the story, ask the reader who gets the carrot in the end.

Fun Activity

Discuss what other animals might like to eat carrots.

Tug! Tug!

Ben has a carrot.

Hop has a carrot.

Ben tugs the carrot.

Hop tugs the carrot.

Ben and Sam tug it.

Hop and Flop tug it.

Ben and Sam and Dad tug it.

Tug! Tug!

Hop and Flop and Lop tug it.

Tug! Tug!

Pop!

They all have carrot.

The Letter S

Trace the lower and upper case letter with a finger. Sound out the letter.

Around, around

Around, around

Some words to familiarise:

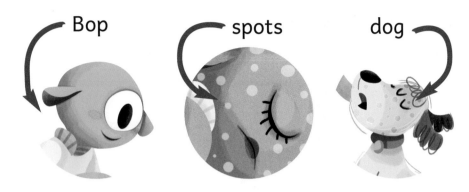

Bop   spots   dog

High-frequency words:

no   and   of

Tips for Reading 'Lots of Spots'

- Practise the words listed above before reading the story.

- If the reader struggles with any of the other words, ask them to look for sounds they know in the word. Encourage them to sound out the words and help them read the words if necessary.

- After reading the story, ask the reader why Bop's mum, dad and dog had lots of spots.

Fun Activity

Count all the spots in the story!

Lots of Spots

Bop's mum had lots of spots.

Bop's dad had lots of spots.

Bop's dog had lots of spots.

Bop had no spots.

Mum had no spots.
Dad had no spots.

Dog had no spots.

Bop had lots of spots!

Book Bands for Guided Reading

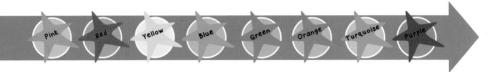

Pink Red Yellow Blue Green Orange Turquoise Purple

Red

Dog in a Dress and Run, Tom, Run!
978-1-84886-290-6

Buzz and Jump! Jump!
978-1-84886-250-0

Bam-Boo and I Wish
978-1-84886-251-7

Sam the Star and Clown Fun!
978-1-84886-288-3

Seeds and Stuck in the Tree
978-1-84886-289-0

Viv the Vet and Top Dog
978-1-84886-347-7

Go Away! and Let's Make A Rocket
978-1-84886-350-7

Catch It, Jess! and Cat Nap
978-1-84886-348-4

Grandad's Cake and Grandad's Pot
978-1-84886-351-4

Zoom! and Come Back, Mack!
978-1-84886-349-1

Plus many more titles in the scheme!

To view the whole Maverick Readers scheme, please visit:

www.maverickbooks.co.uk/early-readers

The Institute of Education book banding system is a scale of colours that reflects the various levels of reading difficulty. The bands are assigned by taking into account the content, the language style, the layout and phonics.

Maverick Early Readers are a bright, attractive range of books covering the pink to purple bands. All of these books have been book banded for guided reading to the industry standard and edited by a leading educational consultant.